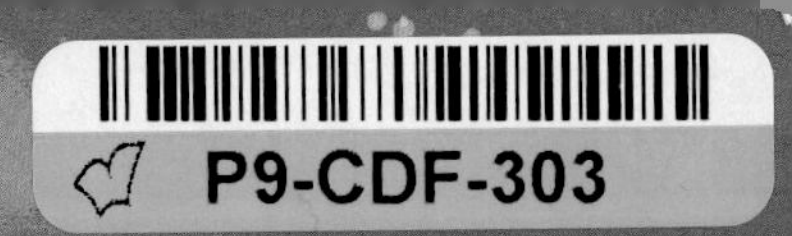
P9-CDF-303

3-Minute

Christmas Stories

publications international, ltd.

Cover illustrated by Richard Bernal
Clock illustrated by Renée Graef
Back cover illustrated by Tom Newsom

Louis Weber, C.E.O.
Publications International, Ltd.
7373 North Cicero Avenue
Lincolnwood, Illinois 60712

Ground Floor, 59 Gloucester Place
London W1U 8JJ

www.pilbooks.com

Manufactured in China.

8 7 6 5 4 3 2 1

ISBN 1-4127-3245-X

CONTENTS

The First Christmas

Written by Leslie Lindecker
Illustrated by Lynda Calvert-Weyant

In the city of Nazareth, in Galilee, there lived a young woman named Mary. She loved God and kept all of the commandments as she was taught. Mary was also very excited. She was going to be married soon to a young man named Joseph.

One day when Mary was praying at home, the angel Gabriel appeared before her. Mary could not speak. She was a little bit frightened by the appearance of this angel.

"Hello, Mary," Gabriel said. "Do not be afraid. God is very pleased with you. In fact, he has chosen you to give birth to his son. You will name the baby Jesus."

"But I am not yet married," Mary said. "How can this be?"

Gabriel said, "The Holy Spirit will come to you. The son born to you will be called the Son of God."

The angel also appeared to Joseph in his dreams that night and said, "Joseph, do not be afraid. The child Mary carries is holy. You will name him Jesus. He will grow up to save his people from all their sins."

The next day, Joseph and Mary were married. They began their life together in Nazareth. Joseph worked as a carpenter, and Mary made their home ready for the new baby.

About eight months later, Joseph learned that he and Mary would have to go to his family's home in Bethlehem. It would be a long, hard trip.

Joseph made Mary as comfortable as he could on their donkey. He walked beside the donkey to guide it on the journey.

Mary and Joseph walked and rode for many days to reach Bethlehem and be counted with Joseph's family.

Night had fallen when they finally reached Bethlehem. Joseph went to find a room at the inn. It was very crowded. Joseph asked for the innkeeper. The man came to the door.

"We need a room for the night," Joseph said.

"We have no rooms!" the innkeeper shouted over the noise in the inn. "See how full we are?"

"Please, sir, my wife could have her baby any minute," Joseph said. "She must rest."

The innkeeper looked at Mary kindly, for he had a very good heart. "You may stay in my stable," he said. "It is not much, but it is warm and dry."

"Thank you, sir," Joseph said.

Joseph walked Mary and the donkey around the inn to the stable.

The innkeeper called out behind them, "There should be plenty of hay and water for your donkey. I will send some food out for you and your wife."

The stable was as crowded as the inn. The innkeeper kept his milk cows and donkeys there. Many people traveling had donkeys in the stalls. Joseph found one stall in the back that was not being used for the animals. Joseph put fresh hay in the stall to make it comfortable for Mary.

Joseph brought fresh water from the well for himself and for Mary and for the donkey. Then he spread their blankets over the hay. Joseph led Mary to the blankets to rest and tethered the donkey to the door of the stall.

Joseph opened the window at the top of the stall so they would have light from the moon and the stars. The innkeeper brought them some bread and cheese to eat. The couple was very thankful for the kindness of the innkeeper.

Mary and Joseph prayed, “Thank you, Lord, for providing shelter for us. Thank you for the blessings you have given us. Thank you for the safe journey you have given us. Amen.”

After making Mary comfortable, Joseph laid down to get some rest.

Late in the night a star began to shine brightly in the sky. Its light shone directly into the small window Joseph had opened in the stall in the stable.

As the star shone its bright light, Mary gave birth to a baby boy. Mary and Joseph looked at the tiny baby with love and joy. They had never seen a more beautiful sight.

"We shall call him Jesus," Joseph said. "It is just as the angel Gabriel said."

In the heavens the angels were singing. In the stable the cooing of a new baby boy was heard.

Even the animals knew that something magical was happening. They gathered in close to see the newborn baby.

Mary and Joseph were beside themselves with happiness. What a beautiful winter night for a healthy baby boy to enter the world!

Mary wrapped Jesus in some clean cloths that she had brought with her on the long journey. Joseph pulled a feeding manger from another stall and filled it with fresh hay. Mary laid the baby in the manger.

The light from the star cast a glow around the stall. All the animals gathered a little closer to look upon the baby.

Mary kissed her new baby boy on the cheek as he slept. She held Joseph's hand. Together, they prayed, thanking God for the miracle of the baby Jesus.

How to Build a Snowman With Your Sister

Written by Kate Hannigan
Illustrated by Keiko Motoyama

Mom told me to play outside today, and that is great. She told me to stay outside as long as I want, and that is great, too. She even told me to build a snowman, and that is the greatest thing of all! I love building snowmen.

But Mom wants me to build a snowman with my little sister! That is not so great.

How can I build a snowman with my little sister when Santa Claus is watching me to see if I am being good? It will be too hard to be good if I have to build a snowman with my little sister.

You see, tomorrow is Christmas! I've been pretty good this year, except for a couple of bad days in July, and I don't want to ruin things. Santa won't remember July, will he?

I'm usually very good when my sister Lizzie isn't around. Lizzie is two, and she needs a lot of help. I don't always like to help. But I guess if Santa Claus is watching, I'll try to be nice.

"Lizzie," I say, "start with a big, round ball of snow like this."

Lizzie begins with a short, square block of snow.

This is going to be a very long day.

Lizzie's not such a bad little sister. It's just that she likes to do everything her own way.

"Lizzie put on top! Lizzie put on top!" she says, holding the snowman's head up in the air.

But Lizzie is too short to reach, and she falls backward into the snow. *Plop!*

"Lou help! Lou help!" she hollers.

We roll another snowball for the head and try again. This time, Lizzie lets me help her. We put the snowman's head on the top together.

"Hooray! Hooray for Lou!" Lizzie shouts, jumping up and down in her red snow boots.

I smile at Lizzie.

Now it's time to put on the snowman's wool scarf and top hat, but Lizzie wants to make it a snow princess. She waves her favorite jeweled crown, feather boa, and some of her other toys.

Lizzie wants a snow princess. I want a snowman like I made last year!

I'm just about to yell at Lizzie when she smiles up at me and starts to sing her favorite Christmas carol. "Here comes Santa Claus! Here comes Santa Claus!"

She's right. Santa Claus is coming—tonight!

"All right," I say to Lizzie, looking around to see if Santa is watching me. "We can make a snow princess."

Once we finish Lizzie's snow princess, we build another snowman for me. It looks great, except Lizzie takes a big bite out of the carrot nose.

I don't even get mad at her. She's been a pretty good helper this time. I can tell that she is trying hard.

"Fun, fun, fun!" Lizzie shouts, clapping her mittens together.

Since I'm being sooooo good, I decide to add a few more things to my list for Santa Claus. I figure it's never too late—Santa probably hasn't even left the North Pole yet.

Lizzie even helps me by letting me use her back for a table. I write a couple of things that I didn't put on my first list because of how bad I was in July.

Lizzie and I run inside to get an envelope for the letter. I take off my snowy boots, but Lizzie just runs ahead of me in her snowy boots.

"Oh, no!" I shout after her. "Lizzie, you're making a big mess!"

Lizzie never listens! Mom said not to track snow into the house, but Lizzie walks all over the nice clean rug. Mom is not going to be happy if she sees this, and Lizzie is too little to clean up. I guess it's up to me to take care of it.

As I clean up the slushy floor, a little voice whispers to me, "Lizzie help Lou."

Now we're ready to play some more. Lizzie and I race back outside in our snow boots, laughing and running through the snow.

But something makes Lizzie stop in her tracks. "Looky, Lou! Looky, Lou!" she shouts.

My snowman—who was perfectly arranged in three round balls of snow just minutes ago—is now a lumpy pile of slush.

Lizzie begins to cry. She is sad for the snowman.

I'm sad, too. I was proud of the work we did together.

Lizzie's snow princess stands in the shade and seems to be holding together all right.

"Poor snowman," Lizzie cries. "Poor Lou. Poor Lou."

Lizzie and I build another snowman near her snow princess. It's in the shade of the house, where the sun isn't shining.

"Snow princess and snowman are friends," Lizzie says. "Just like Lizzie and Lou."

That's right, I think to myself. Just like Lizzie and Lou.

"You did a good job," I say.

It's been a long day, and tonight is Christmas Eve! I take Lizzie's hand, and we go inside. The sooner we get to bed, the sooner Santa will come, and I'm sure Santa has seen how good I've been.

Not everyone knows how to build a snowman with his sister.

A Visit from St. Nicholas

Written by Clement C. Moore
Illustrated by Tom Newsom

’Twas the night before Christmas, when all through the house,
Not a creature was stirring, not even a mouse.

The stockings were hung by the chimney with care,
In hopes that St. Nicholas soon would be there.

The children were nestled all snug in their beds,
While visions of sugarplums danced in their heads;

And mamma in her ’kerchief, and I in my cap,
Had just settled down for a long winter’s nap,

When out on the lawn there arose such a clatter,
I sprang from the bed to see what was the matter.

Away to the window I flew like a flash,
Tore open the shutter and threw up the sash.

When what to my wondering eyes should appear,
But a miniature sleigh and eight tiny reindeer,

With a little old driver, so lively and quick,
I knew in a moment it must be St. Nick!

"Now, Dasher! Now, Dancer! Now, Prancer and Vixen!
On, Comet! On, Cupid! On, Donder and Blitzen!

To the top of the porch, to the top of the wall,
Now, dash away, dash away, dash away all!"

So up to the housetop the coursers they flew,
With a sleigh full of toys and St. Nicholas, too.

And then, in a twinkling, I heard on the roof
The prancing and pawing of each little hoof.

As I drew in my head and was turning around,
Down the chimney St. Nicholas came with a bound.

He was dressed all in fur, from his head to his foot,
And his clothes were all tarnished with ashes and soot.

A bundle of toys he had flung on his back,
And he looked like a peddler just opening his pack.

His eyes, how they twinkled! His dimples, how merry!
His cheeks were like roses! His nose like a cherry!

His droll little mouth was drawn up like a bow,
And the beard of his chin was as white as the snow.

He had a broad face and a little round belly,
That shook, when he laughed, like a bowlful of jelly.

He was chubby and plump, a right jolly old elf,
And I laughed when I saw him, in spite of myself.

He spoke not a word, but went straight to his work,
And filled all the stockings, then turned with a jerk,

And laying his finger aside of his nose,
And giving a nod, up the chimney he rose.

He sprang to his sleigh, to his team gave a whistle,
And away they all flew like the down of a thistle.

But I heard him exclaim, as he drove out of sight,
"Happy Christmas to all, and to all a good night!"

Santa's Gifts

Written by Amy Adair
Illustrated by Kathy Couri

I will tell you about Santa Claus and the way he leaves his magical gifts.

Every Christmas Eve, Santa Claus sets out on a long journey. It is every child's wish to catch sight of Santa Claus, but it is rare that a child ever sees him.

It is while good children are sleeping that Santa Claus leaves his magical gifts for them to find on Christmas morning.

Last Christmas Eve, Rooster was tucked into his comfy little bed. He hoped that Santa Claus would bring him exactly what he had asked for.

Rooster dreamed about Santa Claus and the eight reindeer stopping at his house. In the dream, he woke up to find that Santa had eaten the cookies and drank the milk that he had left out for him. Only a few crumbs remained on the plate. Then Rooster dreamed that he found his stocking filled with lots of little treats, toys, and candy. Then in the dream, Rooster turned and looked under the Christmas tree and discovered that Santa had left him exactly what he had wanted.

Like in his dream, Rooster awoke on Christmas morning to a *ring, ring, ringing.* He rubbed his eyes and saw his gift.

"Cock-a-doodle-do," he sang. "Thank you for the alarm clock, Santa!"

Santa knows just the right gift for every child. In a little cottage tucked in a forest, Baby Bear slept soundly. He dreamed of all the toys and goodies that Santa would bring.

Like many little children, Baby Bear tried to stay awake for Santa. He climbed out of bed and peered out the window at the twinkling stars. He hoped to spot Santa's sleigh, but he finally drifted off to sleep.

Many hours later, when Santa arrived, he tucked a cuddly teddy bear under Baby Bear's arm.

"Sweet dreams, Baby Bear," Santa whispered.

Squirrel woke up very early on Christmas morning. She found a nutcracker.

"Thank you, Santa!" Squirrel exclaimed. "It's just what I wanted!"

Squirrel was so excited about her gift that she almost forgot about her dream. She had dreamed that she heard the *clickety, clickety, clack* of reindeer hooves up on the roof. Then she heard "Ho! Ho! Ho!" In her dream, she peeked out from under her snuggly warm covers and saw a jolly man in a red coat and a red hat. Although she wasn't sure, she thought she saw him leave her the very present she had asked for.

Squirrel thought it was just a dream, but it was a dream come true!

Santa Claus spends the entire night flying from here to there, delivering the perfect gifts. He visits lots of houses, but he always knows just what to deliver to each child.

Santa knew just what Zebra wanted, too. Zebra got up very early on Christmas morning. She was excited to see if Santa had paid her a visit. She rubbed her eyes and found a gift just for her.

"Santa came!" Zebra exclaimed.

She ripped the paper off her present. It was a polka-dot sweater, and it was just the right size.

"Thank you, Santa," Zebra said, slipping on her new sweater.

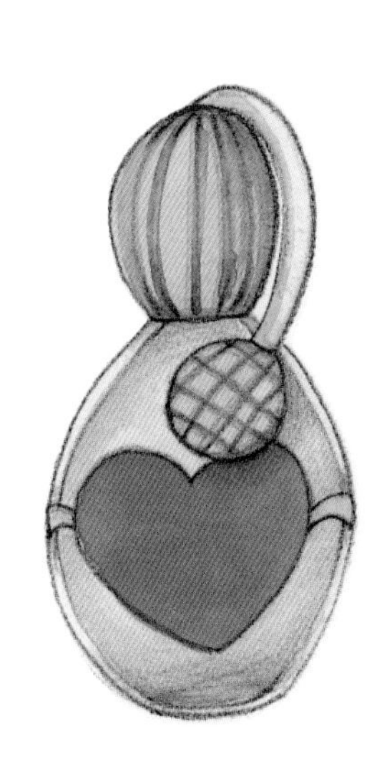

In another house not too far away, Skunk woke up. She scurried out of bed and ran down the steps to see what gift Santa had left.

First, she saw that all the cookies she had made for Santa and the reindeer had been eaten. Not even a crumb was left. Then she saw a gift next to the empty plate.

"What could it be?" Skunk wondered.

She quickly unwrapped her present. Inside was a bottle of sweet-smelling perfume. She sprayed it on.

"It smells so nice," she said. "I love it!"

All over the world children were very happy with the gifts that Santa had left.

Rabbit spent the entire night tossing, turning, and dreaming about Santa. He could barely wait for morning. When it finally came, he leaped out of bed.

Bounce, bounce, bounce! Rabbit bounded down the steps right to the Christmas tree. He unwrapped his gift from Santa. It was a brand-new, shiny pogo stick!

"It's just what I've always wanted!" Rabbit exclaimed. He bounced higher than he had ever bounced before. It was the best gift he had ever received.

The night was growing long for Santa. He had already made a lot of stops.

Ant's house was the last stop on Santa's list. He had one gift left, and it was just for Ant.

In the morning, Ant found a picnic basket. "What a perfect gift!" Ant exclaimed. "It is exactly what I wished for!"

Santa's work was all done.

But Santa Claus will be back again this year with another sleigh full of magical gifts. Maybe you will dream about him in your dreams, and maybe you will find the perfect gift that he left for you.

The Christmas Star

Written by Leslie Lindecker
Illustrated by Joel Snyder

Isaac was glad his father thought he was old enough to help tend the sheep in their pasture. He liked to sit out under the stars in the night sky.

Isaac laughed when his dog raced among the sheep to keep them together. His dog was very loyal and did a good job of keeping the sheep in order, but the dog also looked very silly when he ran.

When the hour got late, Isaac started to get tired. He scratched his dog's head, and soon the dog was asleep. Then Isaac nodded off, too. It was hard for a boy of ten to stay awake all night.

The dog woke up and licked Isaac's face. Isaac awoke with a start.

"What? Oh, good boy," Isaac said. He rubbed his eyes and stretched. It was a very quiet night. The sky was clear and full of stars. It was beautiful and peaceful.

Isaac's father and uncle came to check on him. Isaac was very hungry, and he was glad that the men had brought some food. The three of them shared a loaf of bread and some cheese.

Suddenly, a bright light washed over the shepherds from above. This was a strange happening, and they were frightened. They looked up to see a beautiful angel, and the angel spoke to them.

"Do not be afraid," the angel said. "I bring you good news of great joy!"

The angel explained to the shepherds, "Today a savior is born in Bethlehem. He is Christ the Lord. Go to the city. You will find the baby lying in a manger. Follow the star."

Then in the sky above, hundreds of beautiful golden angels appeared. They sang praises to God. They sang for peace on earth. They sang of miracles. But then, as suddenly as they had appeared, the angels returned to heaven.

As the shepherds looked up at the night sky, they saw a bright, shining star. This star would guide them to the newborn Savior.

The shepherds were amazed by the beauty of the singing golden angels. They knew what they must do.

"We must go to the city and find the Savior," Isaac's father said.

"We must go where the star is shining," Isaac's uncle said as he gazed at the night sky.

"We must hurry!" said Isaac.

The shepherds began to round up their flocks and herd them toward home.

Once the sheep were penned up, Isaac, his father, and his uncle walked toward Bethlehem in search of the newborn Savior that the angel had told them about. The three shepherds knew this was a special day.

Isaac, his father, and his uncle walked through the night. They came to the town of Bethlehem. The star was shining down upon a stable behind an inn in town. The shepherds found Mary, Joseph, and the baby in the stable. Jesus was bundled in clean cloths and was sleeping in a manger full of fresh hay.

The light from the star shone on the baby's face. The shepherds fell to their knees. Isaac knelt by the manger and said a prayer, thanking God for giving the world a savior.

Isaac's father thanked Mary and Joseph for letting them see the baby. When they left, they told everyone they saw about the miracle they had seen.

Every day Isaac did his chores and thought about the baby Jesus. He also thought about what the angel had said. Every night he asked people passing by the fields if they were following the star to see the newborn King of Kings.

The star shone over Bethlehem day and night. Isaac watched the bright star and wondered about the baby as he watched the flocks.

One night, a large camel caravan went past the field. Isaac ran to the edge of the field and called out to the weary travellers.

The caravan stopped, and three men came to speak with Isaac.

"Did you see the one they call Jesus?" Isaac asked.

"We did," one of the men said.

These men were different from any men Isaac had ever seen. They seemed very wise. They wore fancy robes of the finest kinds of cloth.

"We saw the star from our different countries very far away," the man said. He gestured broadly as he spoke. "We have traveled a long time to see this child called the Savior. The kings from our countries sent us with precious gifts to give to him."

The tallest man said, "We asked King Herod where to find this King of Kings. He did not know but told us to return and tell him so that he might worship him also."

"We followed the star to where young Jesus was staying," said the shortest man. "Then I gave him my gift of gold."

"And I gave my gift of frankincense, to scent the air," said the tallest man.

"And I gave my gift of myrrh, a costly oil," said the first man.

"Then in our dreams, we were warned by an angel not to tell Herod where the baby is but to return home another way," said the shortest man. "Now we have met you, my young friend."

"I'm Isaac," Isaac said. "I'm telling everyone about God's glorious star lighting up the sky to show the way to the King of Kings."

Christmas Angel

Written by Leslie Lindecker
Illustrated by Laura Rader

Angelica frowned down at Arnie and fluffed her wings. “Arnie!” she said. “Stop laughing! How will you ever become a proper Christmas angel if you don’t pay attention?”

Arnie hung his little golden head. Then a grin spread across his face, and he looked up at Angelica.

“It’s almost Christmas!” Arnie said. He giggled again. He waved his arms and wiggled his eyebrows and wings. “I am so excited I could fly!”

So he did. Arnie fluttered around in the air while Angelica tried not to laugh at the excited little angel as he did flips and other funny tricks in the air.

“See?” Arnie asked. “I told you I was so excited I could fly!”

Angelica smiled and said, "Arnie, I know you are excited. Do you think you can put all of that good energy into helping the other angels make Christmas wreaths?"

"Sure I can!" Arnie said as he fluttered a few inches off the ground.

Arnie and Angelica went to the wreath workshop. The angels were busy making wreaths of green branches and colored ribbons.

"I can do this!" Arnie said. He zoomed in and out of a wreath, wrapping it with ribbon.

"Aaah! Oops!" Arnie said.

CRASH!

Arnie landed in a tangle of ribbon and branches. Angelica tried not to laugh at his crazy antics.

"It seems as though wreath-making may not be your strongest talent," said Angelica.

"Let's go to the kitchen," Angelica said. "Perhaps making Christmas cookies would suit you better."

"Christmas cookies? Yum!" Arnie said, wiggling his wings as he skipped beside Angelica.

The angels' kitchen was warm. Arnie took a deep breath and rubbed his tummy. The chief baker gave Arnie a spoon and a big, big bowl of cookie batter.

Angelica went back to helping the other angels make Christmas wreaths. She thought that Arnie would be all right helping in the kitchen, but the next time Angelica saw Arnie, he had cookie dough on his face, in his hair, and on his wings. The big, big bowl was empty and his tummy was very full.

"You were supposed to stir the cookie batter, not eat it!" Angelica said with a smile.

Arnie tried to fly up off the floor, but his tummy was too full of cookie batter.

"I must get you away from the kitchen!" Angelica said. "You just might eat everything."

Angelica led the way to the Christmas stocking knitting room.

"Arnie, we must find something you can do to help the Christmas angels!" Angelica said.

"I'm trying," Arnie said with a grin. "See? I can knit Christmas stockings!" He found a pair of knitting needles. Then he sat on the mantle and tried to use the big needles to knit a Christmas stocking.

BING! BANG!

"Can someone help me down?" Arnie asked.

Arnie fell off the mantle and his robe got stuck on a pin meant to hold up a stocking.

"Perhaps making music is something you can do," said Angelica as she helped Arnie down from the pin.

"I can do that!" Arnie said. "I like to sing! I like to drum on things, too."

Angelica and Arnie went to the angels' music room. The angels were singing a beautiful song and playing lovely instruments.

Arnie ran to a harp that was not being played.

"I bet I can play this!" Arnie said as he plinked some of the strings. Then he stretched his arms out in front of him and prepared to play.

SPRING! SPRONG!

The strings popped with a loud noise. The other angels stopped singing and turned to look at him. Arnie was so embarrassed his face turned bright red.

"With your golden hair and that bright red face, maybe color is your talent," Angelica said. "Would you like to try painting some Christmas cards?"

Arnie smiled up at Angelica and lifted his wings. "That would be great!" he said.

They flew to the art room where the artist angels were busily painting and cutting and sprinkling glitter on Christmas cards.

"How pretty!" Arnie said. "I can do this!" He dashed all about, grabbing crayons, paint, and glitter.

CRASH!

With his arms full of crayons, paint, and glitter, Arnie ran into an angel carrying stacks of Christmas cards higher than her head. Angelica cringed as she looked at Arnie and the mess of paint he had created.

"Let's go outside, Arnie," Angelica said. "It will be a lot safer out there."

Arnie skipped and laughed.

"Can I help make the snow?" he asked.

"Hmmmm! That does sound pretty safe," said Angelica. "Let's go over to where the angels make the snow for Christmas."

These busy angels were making a great deal of snow. They made high piles for the snowy places. They made low piles for the not-so-snowy places.

Arnie was very excited. He ran among the piles of Christmas snow.

"I love snow!" Arnie said. "Whoops! Whoa!"

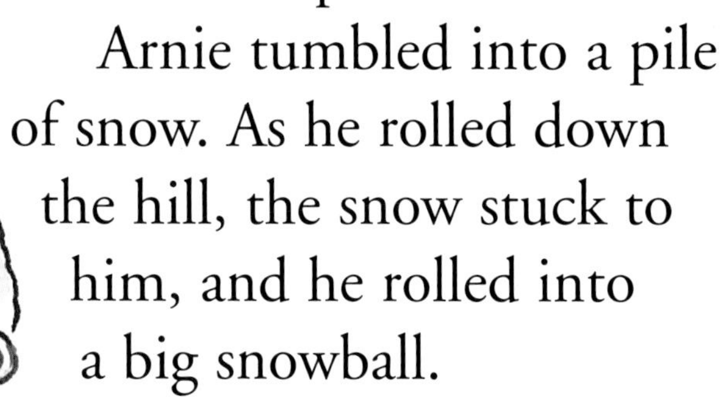

Arnie tumbled into a pile of snow. As he rolled down the hill, the snow stuck to him, and he rolled into a big snowball.

Angelica pulled Arnie out of the snowball, dusted him off, and said, "Let's go look at the Christmas tree the angels put up."

Angelica and Arnie flew hand-in-hand to see the beautiful Christmas tree. It had stars and ribbons and shiny ornaments.

Arnie was so excited about the Christmas tree that he flew straight to the top of it. At the very top of the tree, he began to giggle and wave his arms.

"Arnie, you have found what you can do!" Angelica said proudly. "Every Christmas tree should have an angel at the top!"

The Nutcracker

Adapted by Erin Lyons
Illustrated by Linda Dockey Graves

It was Christmas Eve, and Fritz and his sister Clara could not wait to open their presents. There were so many beautifully wrapped gifts under the tree that they could hardly contain themselves.

Finally, their parents gave the word. The two children rushed to the Christmas tree and began to open the colorful boxes.

Fritz received a toy horse and a set of toy soldiers. Clara received a beautiful doll and a doll-sized bed. They were lovely gifts. Both of the children were very happy with their new toys.

But just when they thought they were finished opening presents, Clara spotted another box behind the tree. Clara asked her mother about the box. It was unlike all the others. It was wrapped in brown paper.

"That's a present from your grandfather," said Clara's mother.

When Clara opened the box and peered inside, her face lit up with delight.

"Look!" she said excitedly. "It's a nutcracker. Isn't he handsome?"

Clara forgot all about her other presents and spent the entire day playing with the nutcracker. She made him walk, talk, and even do a little dance. She would have to remember to write a thank-you note to her grandfather.

The day flew by and suddenly it was time for the children to go to bed. Clara was so tired from all the excitement that she fell asleep right away with the nutcracker in her arms.

Clara woke up suddenly in the middle of the night and realized that the nutcracker was gone! The room was very dark, and Clara thought she saw hundreds of tiny eyes shining in the corners of the room.

Quickly, she lit a candle and was shocked to see that the eyes belonged to hundreds of mice. They were lined up in ranks, just like tiny soldiers, and they were slowly marching toward her.

Leading the little army of mice was one of the oddest sights Clara had ever seen. The leader was the Mouse King, and he had seven heads!

Clara was frozen with fear and about to cry for help when she heard what sounded like a toy trumpet. Then she saw a strange glow from the glass cabinet where Fritz kept his toy army. The toy soldiers had come to life and were marching out of the cabinet. Right there in front of the toy army was her beloved nutcracker!

The nutcracker commanded the army to attack the mice. While the mice and soldiers battled, the Mouse King challenged the nutcracker to a duel.

The nutcracker and the Mouse King battled on and on. Just when it looked as if the Mouse King might win, Clara took off one of her slippers and threw it at the Mouse King. The slipper hit the Mouse King in the heads, and the nutcracker seized the opportunity to defeat him with one final blow.

The whole event was too much for Clara to take, however, and she fainted from fright. When she awoke, the nutcracker was by her side.

"Thank you for saving my life, Clara," the nutcracker said. "By helping me defeat the Mouse King, the spell that turned me into a nutcracker has been broken."

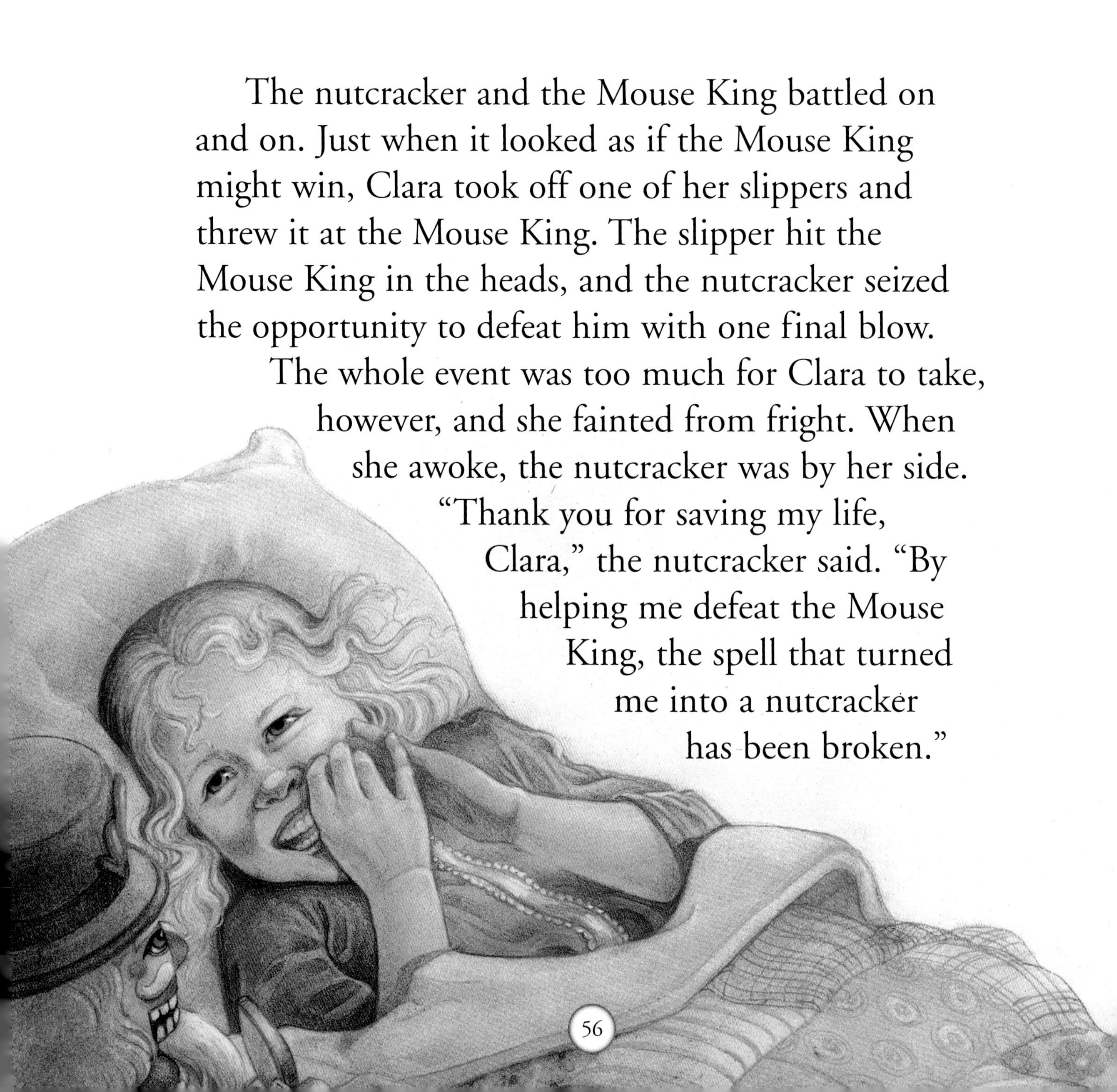

Suddenly the walls of the bedroom magically disappeared. Clara found herself sitting on a beautiful throne in a land where everything was made out of clear crystal sugar and creamy white icing.

When she looked for the nutcracker, she saw he had been transformed into a handsome prince. At her side he said, “My dear Clara, come with me for one night to my home at the Candy Palace. I will show you wonderful things that you have only imagined in your dreams.”

Clara was very excited to see how magical the palace was. Away they went, and soon they came to a lake of sweet, shimmering waters.

They climbed into a swan-boat made of golden caramel and floated magically across the lake to the palace on the other side. There, Clara was greeted by the entire Candy Palace court. The Duke and Duchess of Chocolate presented her with a plate of mouthwatering chocolates. Next, the King and Queen of Coffee and Tea presented her with many splendid gifts wrapped in shiny gold paper. Everything was wonderful.

Then it was time for the grand finale!

The Sugarplum Fairy appeared and performed the most beautiful dance for Clara. Every time her foot touched the ground, sugar flowers and candy jewels sprang up from the ground. And the the night came to an end much too quickly!

"Oh, thank you, Nutcracker Prince," said Clara. "This was the most wonderful night of my life!"

The Nutcracker Prince gave Clara a kiss. Then suddenly, Clara found herself back at home in her bed. She never spoke a word to anyone of her wonderful journey, but she lived happily ever after with her nutcracker always by her side.

Joy to the World

Written by Lisa Harkrader
Illustrated by Linda Howard

A new angel named Holly fluttered her wings nervously. The other angels in her class laughed and flitted around her, but Holly couldn't laugh. She didn't have time.

Holly's class had been learning the meaning of Christmas. Now they had to show what they had learned. The other angels had already passed the test.

"But I can't think of a way to show what I've learned," Holly said.

Holly's friend Ivy showed what she had learned. Ivy visited a family that was decorating for Christmas. The family put up their Christmas tree. They hung their stockings over the fire.

There were plenty of presents under the tree. All of them were wrapped in brightly colored paper. There were even Christmas candles on the mantle.

"Their house was warm and loving," said Ivy, "but they had forgotten something important. The nativity!"

Ivy found the family's nativity in a box in the closet. She rattled the box. Father opened the closet and saw the box. Mother set the stable on a table. The children placed Mary, Joseph, and the animals in the stable. Then they placed baby Jesus on top of the hay in the manger.

"They had forgotten more than the manger," said Ivy. "They had forgotten the reason we celebrate Christmas in the first place. I reminded them!"

Holly's friends Belle and Grace showed what they had learned, too. They visited a day care center. The children there were learning Christmas carols. They played the carols on drums, guitar, and xylophone.

Belle and Grace saw that the children had decorated a Christmas tree.

"Their day care center was festive," said Belle, "but they had forgotten something important."

"They had forgotten to put a star on the top of the tree," Grace said.

Belle and Grace rustled the top of the tree. The children stopped playing their drums and guitar and xylophone. They all stared up at the top of the tree.

"Look!" said one of the children. "The top of the tree is bare. How could we have forgotten such an important part?"

The children got out shiny gold paper. They drew a star and cut it out. Their teacher helped them place the star on the top of the tree.

"They had forgotten more than just a simple star," said Belle.

"They had forgotten that a bright star in the sky led the three wise men to baby Jesus," said Grace. "We reminded them!"

"Belle and Grace passed the test," Holly said to herself. "They helped those children remember the true meaning of Christmas."

Holly's other friends Herbie and Noelle showed what they had learned, too. They visited children who were building a snowman. The children made the snowman with coal, a carrot, and sticks for arms. They put a hat on the snowman's head.

"The children knew how to create something wonderful," said Herbie, "but they had forgotten something else."

"They had forgotten to make snow angels," Noelle said.

Herbie and Noelle fluttered their wings. They swirled the snow beneath them. The children looked up and saw the moving snow.

"Hey!" said one of the children. "This snow is perfect for snow angels!"

The children flopped down in the snow. They waved their arms and legs up and down. They left angel shapes in the snow.

"They had forgotten more than just to make snow angels," said Herbie.

"They had forgotten the angel named Gabriel," said Noelle. "Gabriel told Mary that she would give birth to God's son."

Holly nodded. Everyone had passed the test.

Everyone had passed the test except Holly.

Holly flew over the town, looking for a way to show what she had learned. She heard the children's choir singing carols in the church. The children knew the words and the melodies, but their voices did not seem very happy.

"They have forgotten the joy," said Holly.

Holly fluttered into the church. She hovered just behind the children's choir as they sang. She decided that singing along would be the best way to help.

"Joy to the world!" she sang out.

The children felt Holly's happiness, and everyone in the choir smiled. "Joy to the world!" they sang.

"They knew the words and melody," said Holly, "but they had forgotten the joy. They had forgotten that when baby Jesus was born, a choir of angels appeared before the shepherds. The angels sang out, celebrating the birth of Jesus."

Holly's angel friends sang out with great joy then, too. Holly had passed the test!

"I learned the true meaning of Christmas," said Holly. "I learned how to share it with others."

The Twelve Days of Christmas

Written by Kate Hannigan
Illustrated by Gwen Connelly

During the Christmas season, someone gave me a wonderful gift, but it was not just one gift. It was the gift of twelve days of gifts!

This special someone knows what I love most in the world, so for twelve days, special things arrived at my house to surprise me and make me happy. They arrived one after the other, and it was so much fun!

On the first day, before I knew what was going on, I peeked out my window. Outside I saw a pear tree ripe with beautiful, golden fruit. Perched on one of the branches was a little partridge. It was one of the sweetest things I had ever seen.

Oh! I knew right away who had sent the partridge in the pear tree! It was my special someone. Already it was a wonderful Christmas.

On the second day of Christmas, more birds arrived. That's because my true love knows how much I adore birds—big birds, small birds, short birds, and tall birds. I love birds.

These two were called turtledoves, and they were deeply in love. They spent the day cooing to each other. *Coo-coo, hoo-hoo*, they said back and forth.

They had to join the partridge in the tree to avoid the three French hens who arrived on the third day.

The hens were very excited, and they chased each other around and around the pear tree. Their feathers flew everywhere!

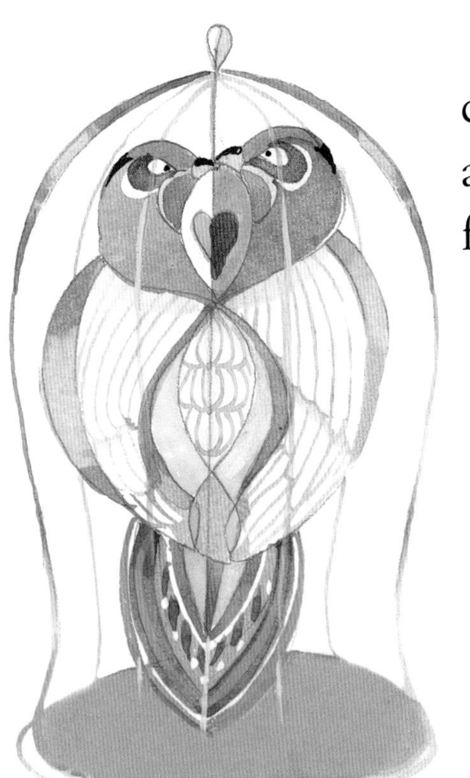

When the four calling birds arrived on the fourth day, things began to get very noisy. *Caw-caw*, they shouted to each other. *Caw-caw!*

My yard was beginning to look and sound like a zoo. So you can imagine my relief when I saw what arrived on the fifth day.

It wasn't a bird. It was jewelry—five golden rings. My true love knows how much I love to play dress-up with my friends and sent enough golden rings for all of us.

I quickly put on one of the golden rings and wiggled my finger. The golden ring sparkled in the bright sunshine, and I smiled. All the birds saw it and seemed to say, *Ooooh! Ooooh!*

When the gift arrived on the sixth day, things got a little crazy. It wasn't more jewelry. It was more birds!

Honk, honk, honk called the six geese as they waddled through the yard. They laid their eggs in my sandbox and under the flowers in Mom's garden.

When the seven swans arrived on the seventh day, the gates of the yard burst open. The birds walked across the street to the park and began to swim in the city pond.

The neighbors walked by and admired all the birds. "Someone must really love you," they said to me. I had to agree.

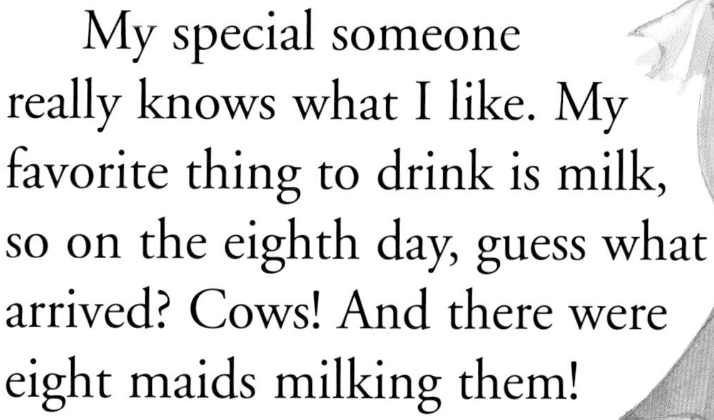

My special someone really knows what I like. My favorite thing to drink is milk, so on the eighth day, guess what arrived? Cows! And there were eight maids milking them!

The cows grazed on the grass in the park, and the maids sat on milk stools next to them. It was a noisy place, with all the birds honking and cooing, and the cows chomping and mooing.

It grew even noisier when the nine dancing ladies came the next day. They clapped their hands as they twirled in their colorful dresses.

The beautiful ladies met their dance partners on the tenth day of Christmas. That's when my special someone sent me ten lords who loved to jump and leap.

The dancers bowed and curtseyed to each other. Then they joined hands and began to celebrate in the street by the park. It quickly turned into a party.

Eleven pipers joined them on the eleventh day, and their music drew my neighbors from their homes. People stood on their porches and listened to the wonderful music.

Everyone joined in the celebration on the twelfth day of Christmas, when the biggest gift of all arrived—the drummers. Cheers erupted as a joyful parade made its way through town.

There were twelve drummers drumming, eleven pipers piping, ten lords a-leaping, nine ladies dancing, eight maids a-milking, seven swans a-swimming, six geese a-laying, five golden rings, four calling birds, three French hens, two turtle doves, and that partridge in the pear tree.

When the parade reached the center of town, my true love was waiting there. The animals and the crowd grew quiet. I could think of only one thing to say: "Thank you!"

The Christmas Cookie Caper

Written by Amy Adair
Illustrated by Jennifer Fitchwell

Derby picked up his red crayon and hummed, "Santa Claus is coming to town."

"What are you doing?" asked Dash. Dash was Derby's little sister.

"I'm writing to Santa Claus," Derby answered, picking up another crayon.

"Can I help?" Dash asked.

Dash always wanted to help, but Derby did not think Dash was very helpful at all. She always made a mess. She always made a mess that he always had to help clean up.

"No, thank you," Derby said politely.

Dash wanted to be just like her big brother. She found a piece of paper, some crayons, and plopped down on the floor next to Derby.

Dash did not know how to spell yet, so she looked over Derby's shoulder and tried to copy the words he had already written.

"What are you doing?" Derby asked, starting to lose his patience.

"I'm writing a letter to Santa Claus," Dash said, smiling. "I just need a little help."

Derby didn't want his sister to copy his letter to Santa. He wanted to keep it a secret.

"I'm all done," Derby said.

He packed up his crayons, folded his letter, and headed to the kitchen. He had work to do.

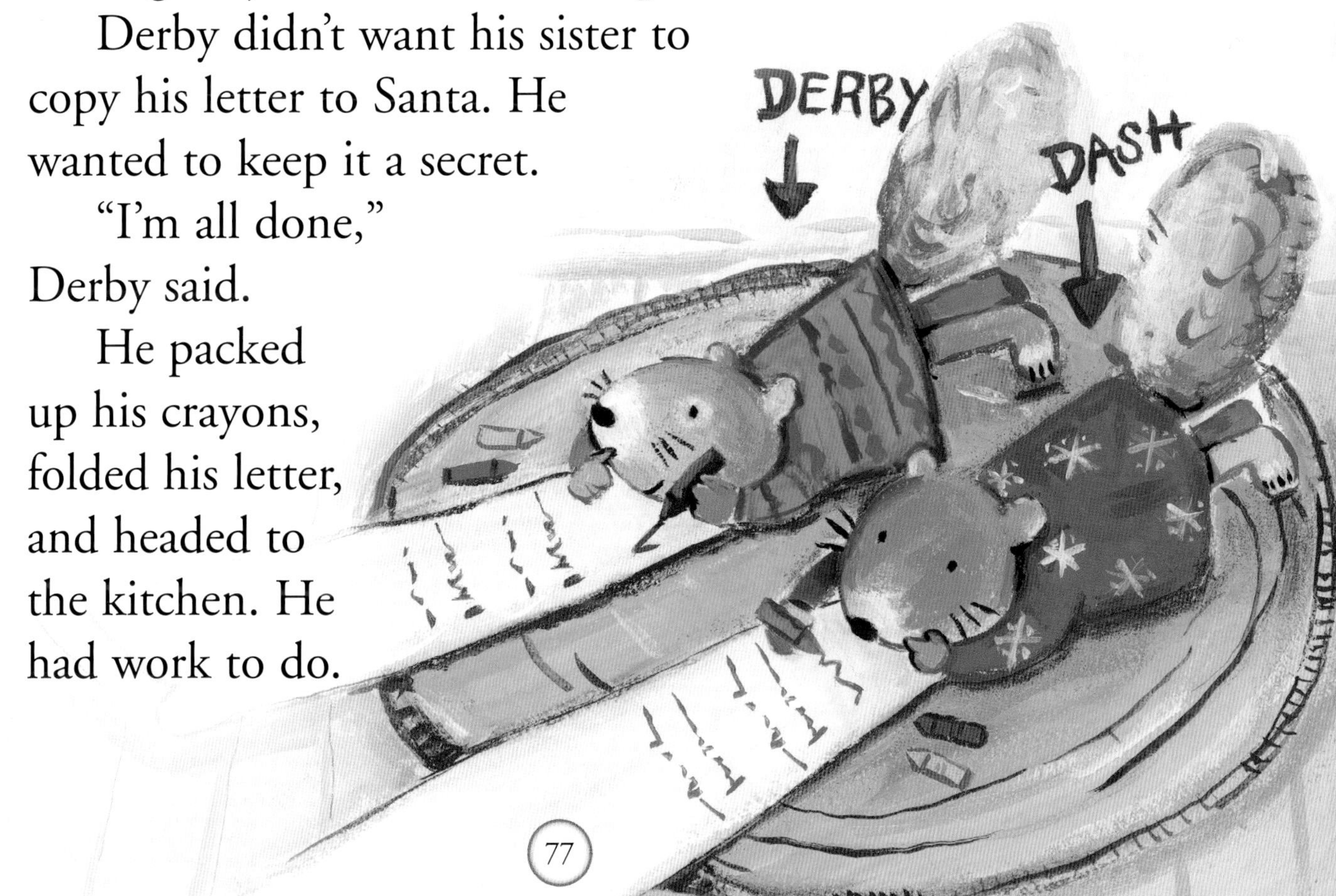

Dash followed Derby into the kitchen. "What are you doing now?" she asked. "Making chocolate chip nut cookies for Santa," Derby said. "Only I can't crack these nuts."

"Can I help?" Dash asked.

Derby was three whole years older than Dash. He did not need help from his little sister. "No, thank you," he said, trying to pry open a nut.

Dash spun around and ran out of the kitchen, but she soon came back. She handed Derby the toy hammer that Santa had left under their Christmas tree last year.

Derby pounded on a nut. *Crack*, went the shell.

"Hey! This actually works!" Derby exclaimed.

Derby saw that his sister really wanted to make cookies with her big brother.

"Would you like to help me?" Derby asked.

Dash nodded her head excitedly. While Derby finished hammering open all the nuts, Dash started cracking the eggs. They were very messy. They splattered all over the place and dripped right on the floor, the walls, and table.

"Uh-oh," Dash said. "I made a big mess. These eggs are everywhere."

"That's okay," Derby said sweetly. "We have lots of eggs."

Derby was surprised by how much he liked working with his little sister. She was having a lot of fun, and he was having a lot of fun, too.

Finally the cookies were done. "Santa is really going to like these," Derby told Dash. "Thank you so much for helping me."

"No problem," Dash said, smiling. "But, um, look at this big mess."

Derby looked around the kitchen. The floor was covered in shells, splattered eggs, and flour. The sink was piled high with dishes, and the counters were completely covered in sugar.

"If we work together we can have this kitchen cleaned up in no time," Derby said, as he strapped sponges onto his feet. He began to skate across the floor, mopping up the mess. Derby suggested that Dash start cleaning the table.

Dash agreed and wasted no time. She started by cleaning the sugar off the table and the countertops. She took a deep breath and with one big blow, all of the sugar flew right off the counter. Derby skated over and mopped it right up.

Then Dash picked up the eggshells that were scattered all around the kitchen floor and tossed them in the garbage can.

Only the dishes were left. Derby washed them while Dash dried. It wasn't long before the kitchen was spotless.

"We did it," Derby said with a big smile. "Santa is going to be so happy when he sees these delicious cookies tonight."

Derby and Dash hadn't noticed that their mom had been standing quietly in the kitchen. She had been watching them the whole time.

"I'm so proud," Mom said. "You worked together. Santa will be very proud, too."

"Do you think Santa would mind if we ate some cookies?" Derby asked.

"I think Santa would love to share his cookies with you," Mom said.

Mom made some hot chocolate and set the table. After everyone ate as many chocolate chip nut cookies as possible, Derby and Dash put the rest on a plate for Santa. Then Derby put his letter next to the plate.

Dash suddenly looked sad. She still didn't have a letter for Santa.

"The cookies are from both of us," Derby said, "so the letter should be from both of us, too."

Derby helped Dash write a new letter.

Dear Santa,

We made chocolate chip nut cookies for you. They taste good, but you should have seen the mess! Don't worry. It was easy to clean up because we worked together to get it done.

Love,
Dash and Derby

The Little Drummer Boy

Written by Leslie Lindecker
Illustrated by Claudine Gévry

David grew up in the inn that belonged to his family.

The inn was one of David's favorite places. His father was the innkeeper and his mother cooked for all the weary travelers who stayed at their inn.

"How is my big boy?" David's father asked as he swung David onto his shoulders.

"Pum pum pum!" David sang as he drummed on his father's head with a pair of wooden spoons.

"We must find this boy a drum or my poor head will not survive!" said David's father as he laughed.

David loved to sing. He sang to his mother as she cooked her delicious meals. He made up songs and banged on pots, pans, and bowls as he sang to her. He banged on everything, but David's mother just smiled at him with encouragement.

"Someday you will sing in the Temple, my son," his mother said. David grinned at his mother.

"Tem tem tem," David sang and drummed on a pot.

David's mother laughed. "Your songs are very beautiful, my son. Keep singing. Your young words and your skillful drumming make my heart happy and my work light. Don't ever stop, my boy."

A few years later, David got a small drum for his birthday. It was a wonderful gift.

"Thank you, Father," David said. He hugged his father's neck. Soon he was beating rhythms on his drum wherever he went.

Pat-a-rum, pat-a-rum, pat-a-rum was how David imitated the sound of the donkeys and carts on the road.

Swish-click-click-tum, swish-click-click-tum was David's brother arranging fresh straw in the horses' stable.

Tic-tic-tic-tonk-tonk, David drummed. This is what he heard when his mother stirred the stew that she was making for the guests at the inn.

David sang about the people who came to the inn. He sang about the horses in the stable. He sang about his family. Everywhere David went, he took his drum with him.

One day, David's father gathered his family together. "We are going to be very busy," he said. "Caesar Augustus declared that a count will be taken of all the families in all of all the towns."

David was a bit confused by what this meant. He asked his father, "Why will this make us busy?"

"People will come here to be counted," David's father said. "They will need a place to stay. They will stay at the inn."

David understood. People who had left their homes to find work elsewhere would return to be counted. On their way home, they would need food and shelter.

David's mother cooked more food. David's sisters cleaned the rooms. David's brother swept out the stable and put new hay and pots of water in the stalls. David's father greeted the people as they came to the inn, and soon the inn was very full. David played his drum and sang his songs for the guests as they waited for their supper.

Late one night, there was a knock on the door. David went to the door with his father. As he held onto his father's robe, he peeked at the young man and his wife who sat on their donkey.

The couple was looking for a place to stay, but there was no room for them at the inn.

David's father was a kind man. "You can stay in the stable," he said. "It is warm and dry. I will send food out to you."

The young man thanked David's father. Then he walked the donkey around to the stable.

David ran to the kitchen, singing a song to his mother. "Come and see! Two people and a donkey! *Pum-pa-rum!*" he said.

David helped his mother carry bread and cheese out to the young couple. His mother told him the woman was going to have a baby soon. "Come back into the house and do not bother her," his mother said.

David was a good boy, and he obeyed his mother. He left the woman alone.

The next day David got up and went to find his mother to see what was for breakfast. When he found her in the kitchen, she said, "The young woman who stayed in the stable last night had her baby."

"The baby is the King of Kings, they say," his father whispered to him. "People are traveling great distances to see the newborn."

"Let's go and see him!" David said.

He and his father walked out to the stable. David was amazed to see how many people were there.

David could not see the baby because of the crowd in the stable. He stood at the back and began to make up a song for the baby. "Come and see the wonders that be," he sang. "A baby born into the world. They bring gifts and come from afar. Just to see the boy who is king."

The crowd parted when they heard David singing. David walked toward the baby and continued to sing his song.

"Little baby, I, too, come to visit you. But I do not have a gift to leave. I am just a boy, and a poor one too. The gift I can give is the sound of my drum and this song. May I play my song for you?"

The baby's mother smiled and nodded. Her husband smiled at David as well. All the while David sang, it seemed as if the stable animals were keeping time with his drum.

Then the baby smiled at David, reached out, and patted his drum.

Jingles All the Way

Written by Amy Adair
Illustrated by Keiko Motoyama

Jingles groaned. It was not a good day. In fact, it was a very bad day.

"The tips of my ears are cold," he grumbled. "My nose is cold. My feet are cold. Today is a very bad day."

Jingles hung his head. He listened to the *crunch, crunch, crunch* of the snow as he pulled the sleigh.

Jingles was delivering a big Christmas tree to Farmer Brown. But Jingles did not want to deliver the tree.

Jingles wanted to play with all of his friends. Instead, he pulled the sleigh up a steep hill. He tripped over a log that was in the middle of the path.

Then Jingles started to cry. He could barely see the path through all his tears.

When Jingles reached the top of the hill, he heard his best friend Baxter laughing and playing.

"Hey, Jingles!" Baxter yelled. "Want to play?"

Jingles shook his head.

"What's wrong?" Baxter asked, climbing out of his snow fort.

"The tree is too heavy, I stubbed my toe, I'm tired, I'm hungry, and I'm never going to get to Farmer Brown's house," Jingles complained to his friend. "Today is a very bad day."

Baxter did not like to see his best friend so upset. He wanted to help Jingles. He scratched his head and thought for a moment.

"What if you rested for a minute?" Baxter asked. "You'll feel better and the sleigh won't seem so heavy."

Jingles rested for a minute. He started to feel a little better, but he still did not want to haul the big Christmas tree all the way to Farmer Brown's house.

"Maybe you need a snack," Baxter suggested. "I'll share mine with you." Baxter handed Jingles some cookies.

"Do you feel better now?" Baxter asked, hopeful.

"Not really," Jingles said as he sighed. "Today is still a very bad day."

"I have an idea," Baxter said, jumping up and down excitedly. "I'll help you pull the sleigh to Farmer Brown's house. Then we can all go sledding together in the sleigh!"

Jingles thought about it for a moment. He imagined flying down a snowy hill in the sleigh. It did sound like a lot of fun.

But then he shook his head. "It won't work," he said sadly. "The sleigh is too heavy for you. This is the worst day ever."

Jingles looked sadder than ever. “It’s no use,” Jingles said. “I’ll just pull the tree to Farmer Brown’s house all by myself. This day can’t get any worse.”

Baxter suddenly had an idea. “Wait here,” he said, then scurried away. Baxter wasn’t gone very long. He came back with lots of friends.

“We’re here to help,” one happily told Jingles.

All of the friends grabbed the reins of the sleigh. “One, two, three, pull!” Baxter yelled.

All the friends worked together to deliver the big Christmas tree. They pulled the sleigh up and down the snowy hills, through the thick woods, and right to Farmer Brown's house.

"Thanks for helping," Jingles said to his friends. "I could not have done it without you. You made me feel much better."

"This sleigh ride isn't over," Baxter said, smiling. "Climb on in, Jingles."

When Jingles was in the sleigh, Baxter and the others pulled Jingles up a hill.

"Look out below!" Baxter yelled as the sleigh, Jingles, and all the friends raced down the hill.

"Wheeeee!" Jingles shouted, happily.

"It's Jingles all the way!" Baxter said.

It turned out that what started as a very bad day was one of the best days ever. Jingles got to spend it with all of his best friends!

The Elves and the Shoemaker

Adapted by Erin Lyons
Illustrated by Kathleen McCord

Once there lived a shoemaker who was very skilled at his work. He made wonderful shoes that everyone loved. However, the shoemaker had grown poor because of hard times in his village. People could no longer afford to buy shoes.

Four days before Christmas, the shoemaker found that he only had enough leather to make one more pair of shoes.

Tired from his worries, the shoemaker left the leather on the worktable and went to bed. He could make a fresh start in the morning. A good night's sleep was just what he needed.

But when morning came, the shoemaker was amazed to find that the finest pair of shoes he had ever seen was sitting on his worktable!

"Who could have done this?" he asked.

The shoemaker showed the shoes to his wife, and she was amazed, too.

Just then, a well-dressed man knocked at the door. He was a rich man passing through the village who needed a new pair of shoes. He spotted the ones in the shoemaker's hands and asked to try them on. The shoes fit him perfectly and looked so handsome that the man paid the shoemaker double the price.

"I'm happy to pay more for such quality work," said the rich man. "You should be proud. These are the finest shoes I've ever worn."

The shoemaker and his wife were so happy that they celebrated as soon as the man left. They even did a dance around the shop. What a lucky day!

With all the money the rich man had given them, the shoemaker's wife was able to buy a nice big ham for dinner. The shoemaker was also able to buy enough leather for two more pairs of shoes.

After their wonderful ham dinner, the shoemaker was too tired to do much work. He decided to cut the leather for the new shoes but wait until the next day to put them together. For now, he left the leather on the table and went to bed.

That night, he dreamed of making the loveliest pair of women's slippers he had ever seen.

The next morning, the shoemaker went to his worktable and rubbed his eyes. There he saw the very shoes he had dreamed about!

"How could this be?" he asked.

The shoemaker and his wife admired the fine craftsmanship of the two pairs of shoes. The shoes had a beautiful design and perfect stitching.

Another customer came into the shop that day. She was a relative of the rich man who had bought the first pair of shoes. The wealthy woman was delighted to find that the new shoes fit her perfectly, and they even matched the new ballgown she had recently purchased. She was so thrilled with her new shoes that she paid the shoemaker double the price.

The shoemaker and his wife could not believe their luck. "It looks like our money troubles are over!" said the shoemaker.

"Now, dear," his wife said, "we don't know how long this will last. We must take care. We must find out what is behind this miracle."

"You are absolutely right, my love," said the shoemaker. "What do you say we stay awake tonight and hide ourselves? Maybe then we can find out who is doing all of this wonderful work for us."

The shoemaker's wife agreed. That night, the shoemaker and his wife hid themselves and kept watch over the worktable.

As the hour approached midnight, the shoemaker and his wife began to get sleepy. Nothing was happening in the shop. But just as the couple began to nod off, something moved in the room!

Two tiny little elves came in through an open window, wearing nothing but tattered rags. They quickly climbed onto the worktable, picked up the shoemaker's tools, and went to work.

The shoemaker and his wife could not believe their eyes! They watched all night, without making a sound, as the little elves stitched and painted perfect shoe after perfect shoe. When they were finished, the elves scurried out of the window just as they had come in, leaving behind their wonderful work.

When the elves were gone, the shoemaker and his wife came out from their hiding spot.

"We must do something nice for the elves to show them our appreciation," said the shoemaker.

"I was thinking the same thing," said his wife. "Did you see how poorly dressed they were? We could make them some new clothes."

"What a wonderful idea!" said the shoemaker.

Without pausing for breakfast, the shoemaker and his wife went straight to work. The shoemaker crafted two tiny pairs of red leather shoes, and his wife sewed a whole set of clothes for each elf. The couple even made new little hats for the elves.

That night was Christmas Eve. The shoemaker and his wife placed their gifts for the elves on the worktable and hid behind the cupboard again. Sure enough, the two elves climbed through the window right at the stroke of midnight.

When the elves found the nice little clothes and shoes waiting for them, they tried them on right away. The clothes fit them perfectly! The happy little elves jumped up and down for joy. They danced all over the room until finally they danced right out of the window.

The shoemaker and his wife never saw the elves again, but they had great success with their own well-made shoes and lived happily ever after.

The Night Before Christmas

Written by Lisa Harkrader
Illustrated by Jayoung Cho

It was Christmas Eve, and Nell, the youngest rabbit, asked, "Can we stay up until Santa comes?"

Nell asked the same question every Christmas, and every Christmas Mama said no. But this time, Mama looked at Papa. Papa looked at Mama. They both nodded, and Mama said, "Okay."

"Hooray!" shouted Nell.

Then seven happy little rabbits danced around the room. There were Nell and Hannah and Emma and Penelope and Will and Jack and Peter.

"The night can be pretty long," said Mama.

"You might get tired of waiting," said Papa.

"We could never get tired of waiting for Santa," said Nell. "We have a million fun things we can do until he comes."

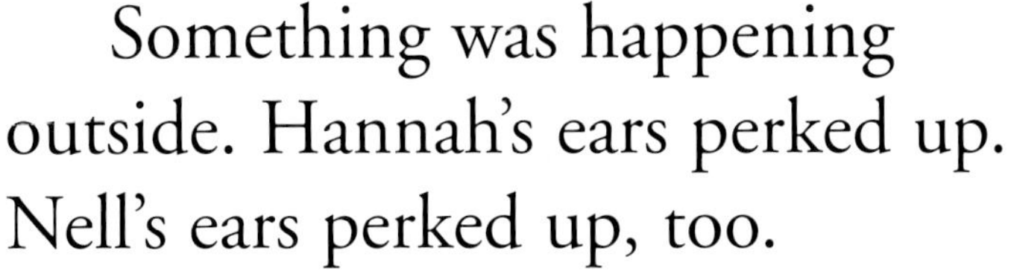

Something was happening outside. Hannah's ears perked up. Nell's ears perked up, too.

Hannah and Nell had heard carolers singing in the street. Nell invited them in and gave them cocoa.

The rabbits gathered 'round as the carolers sang Christmas songs. On the rug sat seven quiet rabbits. There were Nell and Hannah and Emma and Penelope and Will and Jack and Peter.

All the little rabbits were feeling the Christmas spirit more and more.

Soon the carolers left.

"The Christmas songs were lovely," said Mama, "but it's still pretty early."

"You still have a long time to wait for Santa," said Papa.

"And we need lots of time," said Nell. "We have so much to do. We haven't hung our stockings yet."

The seven rabbits hopped up to the attic. They found their Christmas stockings packed in a box. Down the stairs ran seven eager rabbits. There were Nell and Hannah and Emma and Penelope and Will and Jack and Peter.

Papa and the kids hung the stockings over the fire.

"The mantle looks nice," said Mama. "I'm sure Santa will fill your stockings full."

"But it's still a long time until he arrives," said Papa.

"And that's a good thing," said Nell, "because we have lots of baking to do for Christmas dinner."

"Cookies," said Penelope.

"Cake," said Hannah.

"An enormous blackberry pie," said Jack.

Into the kitchen skipped seven cheerful rabbits. There were Nell and Hannah and Emma and Penelope and Will and Jack and Peter.

Peter and Jack baked cookies. Will and Penelope baked a cake. Emma and Hannah made a pie that Nell filled with blackberries.

"Now you'll have delicious goodies for Santa," said Mama.

"It's such a long time until he gets here," said Papa. "I'm sure his tummy will be growling."

"My tummy is growling, too," said Nell.

The other rabbits nodded. They pulled carrots from the refrigerator for a snack. Then out of the kitchen shuffled seven hungry rabbits. There were Nell and Hannah and Emma and Penelope and Will and Jack and Peter.

The rabbits nibbled their carrots.

"You're all very quiet," said Mama.

"Maybe you're getting tired," said Papa.

"We can't be tired," said Nell. "Santa Claus hasn't arrived yet."

Mama pulled Nell onto her lap and gathered the other rabbits around her. "You've stayed up very late," she said with a soft, tender voice. "You've had lots of fun, but now I think it's time to go to bed."

"You said we could wait for Santa," said Nell. "You said we could stay up!"

"You promised!" wailed Nell and Hannah and Emma and Penelope and Will and Jack and Peter.

Mama looked at Papa. Papa looked at Mama.

"I guess we did promise they could wait for Santa," said Mama.

"And we'll keep our promise," said Papa, "but I think we should wait upstairs in bed. Santa won't want us to disturb him while he's filling the stockings and putting gifts under the tree."

"I guess that would be okay," said Nell. "We can tell each other Christmas stories in bed."

The rabbit family trudged upstairs. Mama and Papa tucked their seven little rabbits into bed. They kissed each one on the nose.

"Have fun telling your stories," said Mama.

"And whatever you do, don't fall asleep," said Papa with a smile.

All cozy and telling Christmas stories were seven little rabbits. There were Nell and Hannah and Emma and Penelope and Will and Jack and Peter.

Nell and her siblings were getting tired. "We can't fall asleep," she said. "We have to wait for Santa."

Mama and Papa tiptoed to the door and turned off the light. Under the covers snuggled seven snoring rabbits. There were Nell and Hannah and Emma and Penelope and Will and Jack and Peter.

The Gift of the Magi

Adapted by Erin Lyons
Illustrated by Wendy Edelson

It was Christmas Eve and Della was crying. She had only been able to save one dollar and twenty cents this year, and she had not yet bought a Christmas present for her beloved husband Jim.

Della knew that even though Jim didn't have very much money either, he would still get her a wonderful Christmas present.

Jim and Della had met a long time ago and had been in love for years, but times were difficult for the young couple. Money was not an easy thing to come by.

Della knew that she had to come up with a solution. She wanted nothing more in this world than to make Jim happy on Christmas.

Della paced around the living room trying to think of what to do. Then she caught sight of herself in the mirror.

Della stopped and admired her long hair. She had the most beautiful hair in the whole town. Everyone knew it was her most prized possession.

Della had been letting her hair grow long since she was a young girl. Her luxurious locks were a source of much pride for Della.

As much as she loved her hair though, she loved Jim more.

Suddenly, Della had an idea. She went to the closet and grabbed her tattered red coat and old hat. Her lip trembled a little because she was sad about what she had to do. But then she thought of Jim again and a smile lit up her face.

Quickly, she left the house and went down the street. It was a beautiful, sunny winter afternoon. There were many families out doing some last-minute shopping for Christmas gifts. Children were playing games in the snow. Della smiled and waved at the faces she recognized as she walked down the street.

Finally, Della reached her destination. She stopped at a small store with a sign over the door that read “Miss Margaret’s Wigs.” Della closed her eyes, took a deep breath, and walked inside.

Miss Margaret was busy brushing some new wigs that she had just put on display. When Miss Margaret looked up to see who had entered her store, she was surprised to see Della. But before Miss Margaret could say anything, Della asked, “How much will you pay for my hair?”

“How does twenty dollars sound?” Miss Margaret quietly asked.

“You may take all of it,” Della said. Then she sat down in the cutting chair.

Margaret went to work without a single word.

It didn't take long for Miss Margaret to cut off all of Della's beautiful hair.

"This will truly make the most gorgeous wig, Della," said Miss Margaret.

With the twenty dollars, Della went straight to the department store. She searched for hours for the perfect gift for Jim and finally found just the thing. It was a lovely gold chain for his watch. The watch had belonged to Jim's grandfather and was the most precious thing Jim owned. She was overjoyed with her purchase.

Della rushed home and tried to style her short hair in the mirror before Jim came home. It was difficult, but she managed. She hoped that Jim would still think she was pretty, even without her long hair.

At exactly 5:30 that evening, Jim walked in the door. When he saw Della, he froze with a look of shock on his face.

"Jim, darling, I sold my hair to buy your Christmas present," Della said softly. Jim still looked shocked. "Don't worry—it will grow back," said Della.

"Oh, it's not that, darling. You are still my beautiful Della. It's just that ... well, here." Jim pulled a small present out of his coat and gave it to Della.

Della could not believe her eyes when she opened the box. She found three jeweled hair combs inside, and she burst into tears.

"Oh, Jim!" Della said. "These are the combs I've wanted since last year!" Her tears were of both happiness and sadness, but they were also of love. Suddenly, she remembered her present for Jim.

Della reached into her pocket and pulled out the box with the gold watch-chain in it. When Jim opened it, his face became sad.

"Thank you, darling," Jim said. "You are wonderful, but I sold my watch so that I could buy you the combs."

Jim and Della embraced each other. The love they felt for one another was tremendous.

"Oh, Jim, I can't believe this," said Della. As she said this she looked up at him and smiled.

"My sweet Della," Jim whispered back to her, "we are truly a well-matched pair, aren't we?"

"Yes, my darling," Della said. "We are the best pair in the whole town."

"I have a feeling this will be a Christmas that we will not soon forget," said Jim. "Our children and our grandchildren will enjoy hearing this story for years to come."

Though they were both a little sad, Della and Jim felt more in love than ever before.

Jim was reminded of the Christmas story of the three wise Magi who traveled so far to give the baby Jesus their precious gifts. Della thought it was a fitting story to recall. She and Jim had given each other very precious gifts. The best part of Christmas was the giving.

As Della and Jim held each other closely, they knew it was a very special Christmas.

Barnyard Christmas

Written by Guy Davis
Illustrated by Laura Rader

Parker Pig listened to the holiday carols coming from Farmer Grant's house. He enjoyed the lights dangling from the farmhouse and the star shining on top of the Christmas tree in the window.

"Tomorrow is Christmas," oinked Parker Pig to Helen Horse. "It's my very favorite holiday! Look how beautiful Farmer Grant's farmhouse is! We need to do something like that to dress up our barnyard for the holiday."

"That's a wonderful idea!" neighed Helen Horse. "Let's build a snowman!"

So Parker Pig and Helen Horse rolled a large ball of snow for the snowman's body. Then they rolled a smaller ball of snow for the snowman's head.

"What are you doing?" grunted Gregory Goat.

"We're building a snowman," oinked Parker Pig. "We are decorating the barnyard for Christmas!"

Gregory Goat stamped his hooves excitedly. "I want to help with the snowman, too!" he grunted.

He ran over to the woodpile and pulled out two long sticks.

"The snowman needs arms!" grunted Gregory Goat.

"Excellent!" neighed Helen Horse.

"Brilliant!" oinked Parker Pig.

"We want to help, too!" thumped Betsy and Bobby Bunny.

"Do you have any ideas about how to decorate our barnyard snowman?" oinked Parker Pig.

"We sure do!" thumped the twin bunnies. They hopped about the barnyard until they found what they were looking for—a pile of crunchy carrots.

"Carrots?" grunted Gregory Goat. "What are your little bunny brains thinking? What does a snowman need with carrots?"

"Watch this!" thumped Betsy Bunny. She hopped on Bobby Bunny's back. Then she stuck a carrot into the snowman's face.

"It's a nose for the snowman!" thumped Bobby Bunny.

Gregory Goat grunted and grinned.

Parker Pig stepped back and admired their work. "We need something to keep the snowman's head warm," he oinked.

Claire Crow was sitting up in the barn's rafters. "I know just what you need," cawed Claire Crow. She quickly flew out of the barn and into the cornfield.

Claire Crow landed on the scarecrow's shoulder. "I'd like to borrow your hat, Mr. Scarecrow," she cawed. Mr. Scarecrow gave her a wink and off she flew with his festive hat.

Helen Horse neighed happily as Claire Crow flew back into the barnyard and dropped the hat on the snowman's head. The hat looked perfect on the snowman!

"We want to help, too!" purred two little voices.

All of the animals looked around.

"Who said that?" oinked Parker Pig.

"We did," purred Krissy and Karl Kitty, peeking out of a haystack. "We want to help decorate the snowman for Christmas, too!"

Parker Pig smiled down at the two kittens.

"Do you have something to share with us?" Parker Pig oinked.

"Yes, we do," purred the kittens. "We found some really great mittens and a neat scarf, and we want to share them with the snowman!"

All the animals smiled as the two kittens placed the mittens on the snowman.

"Perfect!" they all shouted together.

"Our barnyard snowman looks terrific!" oinked Parker Pig. "But he still needs something else."

"That's where I can help!" squeaked another voice from the rafters.

"Who said that?" purred Krissy Kitty, looking up.

"It's me," squeaked Mel Mouse, climbing down from the rafters. "I may be small, but I can see exactly what the snowman needs!"

Mel Mouse scampered across the barnyard and placed two blue buttons on the snowman for eyes.

"See?" squeaked Mel Mouse proudly. "I told you I could help!"

The animals all agreed and stamped their feet happily.

Everyone was very excited about the snowman, but there was one barnyard animal who wasn't very happy. Stephanie Squirrel had seen all of the activity from her nearby oak tree. She really wanted to help decorate the snowman, but she had nothing to share.

"I really would like to give something, but I don't have anything like a hat or a carrot or buttons," chattered Stephanie Squirrel, sadly. "I have nothing to give to make the snowman better."

Then an idea came to her! She quickly climbed to where her acorns were stored for the winter.

Grabbing a few of her precious acorns, Stephanie Squirrel scampered across the barnyard. She climbed up on the snowman and gave him three acorn buttons.

Stephanie Squirrel stepped back and smiled proudly. Mr. Snowman was complete!

"Thank you, everyone," oinked Parker Pig. "Your gifts have made our barnyard very merry...and just in time for Christmas!"

The animals gathered around Mr. Snowman and were happy with their work. Now that the barnyard was decorated, it would be the best Christmas ever!

The Friendly Beasts

Written by Kate Hannigan
Illustrated by Linda Dockey Graves

Long ago in the town of Bethlehem, on a cold winter's night, a baby was born in a stable.

The friendly beasts who lived there — the donkey, the cow, the sheep, and the birds — watched over the tiny baby. They watched him sleep peacefully. When the tiny baby woke up, the animals huddled very close to keep him warm. The animals knew it was a special night. They knew the baby was special, too.

"We will tell the story to our children, and they will tell their children," they said.

The donkey was the first to share his story with the other animals. They listened closely.

The donkey explained how the journey across the sandy desert to Bethlehem was long and difficult. The donkey had leaned into the whipping wind and climbed up steep hills.

"I carried Mary on my back," the donkey said, "and Joseph walked at my side."

When they finally reached the town, Mary and Joseph searched for a place to spend the night, but there was no room for them at the inn.

"They had to stay in the stable with us," the donkey said. "All the animals gladly made room for them."

Then the cow told her story. She had just settled in to eat her dinner when she heard the donkey's *heee-haw* in the quiet night. She watched Joseph help Mary climb down from the donkey's back.

The travelers looked weary, but there were no beds to sleep on and no covers to keep them warm. There was only hay in the stable.

"When the baby was born," said the cow with a swish of her tail, "I gave Mary my manger to use as a cradle for the baby."

Mary wrapped the baby in swaddling clothes and laid him in the manger full of soft hay. She and Joseph were very tired from their journey, but they were not ready to leave the baby's side. Along with the animals, they gazed at the infant as he slept.

Little did Mary and Joseph know that a brilliant star lit up the night sky outside the stable. An angel was also there, hovering gracefully overhead.

As Mary rocked the sleeping baby in her arms, the cow and the donkey greeted three camels arriving from distant lands.

"We carried three kings," said the camels. "They were wise men who brought wonderful gifts to lay before the child."

The camels told the other friendly beasts all about their long journey. They told of how the bright star in the night sky was their guide. They told how the star showed them the way to the stable and to the baby.

Not long after the camels arrived, the animals heard a faint *baa, baa, baa* echoing softly outside in the cold night air.

The sound grew louder until the cow and donkey finally saw the fluffy white coats of the sheep drifting like clouds toward the stable.

The shepherds who tended the flock were with the sheep. They carried bundles of blankets for Mary, Joseph, and the baby. The blankets were made from the woolly coats of the sheep. The shepherds had sheared the sheep the previous spring and had made blankets from the wool. The blankets made wonderful gifts for the baby.

"I kept the baby warm with my thick woolly coat," the sheep said.

All the animals in the stable knew that they had provided something to help Mary, Joseph, and the beautiful new baby. They were very proud.

Then more visitors came to the stable and brought many fine gifts for the baby. That is when the birds gave the most beautiful gift of all.

Perched on a wooden beam above the manger where the baby slept, the birds sang a sweet song that filled the air.

"Our song made the baby happy," the birds said. "He smiled at us."

As all the animals in the stable gathered around the baby, they knew it was a very special night. It was the night when Christ the Savior was born.

Christmas Puppy

Written by Guy Davis
Illustrated by Jane Maday

Santa Claus laughed as he chased the new puppies around his workshop. Santa loved to play with puppies. Now that his dog Belle had a new litter, Santa had lots of puppies to play with. In fact, he had twelve new puppies to play with!

"Ho, ho, ho!" Santa said as he picked up one of the little barking pups. "You will be Jolly, and these two puppies are your sisters, Holly and Dolly."

The puppies were everywhere. One elf even found a puppy hiding in an empty Christmas present box.

The puppies liked to play and frolic. One of them was playing hide-and-seek with his mother, Belle. Belle found the puppy hiding in one of Santa's red hats.

Another of the puppies played with a jack-in-the-box while one of his sisters played in a big basket of yarn.

The little puppies even ran outside and back inside through a little doggie-door that Santa had built into the big door of his workshop.

Santa felt great joy while he watched Belle's puppies play around the workshop. All of the elves loved the puppies, too. They took lots of breaks from making toys to play with the puppies and to get them food.

Santa is very good with names. He was proud of all the names he had given to his eight reindeer. He was going to enjoy naming all of Belle's puppies, too. He called each of the puppies to him.

"I see Twinkle and Winkle, and Jingle and Jangle, and Bingle and Bangle, and Poppy and Floppy, and...," Santa paused. "Where is little Pepper?"

The elves stopped working to help Santa search for Pepper. They looked under toys and inside of gift boxes, but they couldn't find little Pepper anywhere.

Suddenly, Santa heard a little yelp.

"Well, there you are!" said Santa. The little puppy had fallen into a box of Santa's letters from good girls and boys around the world. Pepper leapt out of the box and into Santa's arms.

Santa smiled and hugged the puppy close. "You must be more careful, little Pepper," said Santa. "We don't want to lose you. What's a little puppy like you doing in a big box of letters like that, anyway?"

Pepper gave Santa several affectionate puppy kisses and then hopped back into the box of letters.

"Well, I'll be," said Santa, scratching his head. "Are you trying to show me something, Pepper?"

Pepper barked loudly and pawed at one of the letters. Santa picked it up and read it.

The letter was from a little girl named Katie. The letter said that Katie lived in Wyoming. She was the youngest child in a family where the older children had left for college. She really missed her brothers and sisters and was very lonely.

Santa put on his reading glasses and sat down to read Katie's letter out loud to Pepper.

Dear Santa,

All I want for Christmas is a pet so I will have someone to play with. Thank you!

Love,
Katie

When he was done reading, Santa smiled at Pepper. "Good dog, Pepper!" he said. "I think you will make the perfect pet for a certain little girl."

On Christmas Eve, Pepper climbed up into Santa's sleigh. All of Pepper's siblings wanted to come along to say good-bye to little Pepper.

"Sure you can come," said Santa. "The more the merrier! Hop on in!"

All the puppies jumped on board, and Santa's sleigh took off to deliver presents to children around the world. Later that evening, Santa's sleigh headed toward Wyoming. Pepper became very excited!

After they landed at Katie's farm, Santa said good-bye to little Pepper.

"You're a good dog, Pepper," said Santa, hugging the puppy close. "We will miss you at the North Pole, but you will make this little girl very happy."

Pepper gave Santa a big, slobbery kiss. Then Pepper said good-bye to all his brothers and sisters.

The next morning was Christmas. Wearing a great big bow, Pepper sat quietly under the Christmas tree. But as soon as Katie started running down the stairs, Pepper's tail started wagging.

Katie stopped at the bottom of the stairs when she spotted Pepper sitting under the tree. A huge smile came over her face.

"A puppy!" cried Katie. "It's exactly what I wanted! Thank you, Santa!"

Pepper jumped into Katie's arms. Pepper got exactly what he wanted, too!

The two new friends ran outside to play in the snow together. They ran, jumped, and rolled around in the snow while Pepper gave Katie affectionate doggie kisses. It was the best Christmas ever!

A Christmas Miracle

Written by Lisa Harkrader
Illustrated by Kathleen McCord

Rose peered out the window, searching the clear night sky for a shooting star. Christmas was only three days away, and Rose had to make a wish. She wanted to give so much to her family, but she would need the help of a Christmas miracle.

"Time for bed," Rose's mama said.

Rose's brothers, James and Henry, were settling onto their mattresses near the warm fire. Baby Bonnie was already fast asleep in her makeshift bed—a drawer lined with blankets.

Rose crawled into the bed she shared with her sister Sarah.

Rose couldn't sleep. She didn't want to give her family homemade Christmas presents again this year. She wanted to give Mama the beautiful green dress in the window of Mr. Pranger's store. She wanted to give Papa a shiny new black pipe. She wanted to give Bonnie a crib, the boys new wool coats, and Sarah a dapple-gray pony.

Rose sneaked another peek out the window. "I want to give them the gifts they truly want," she said to the night sky. "It's only a dream, but I wish it could come true."

Rose smiled at the thought of her family before she crawled under the covers and went to sleep.

The next morning, Rose helped her mother wash the dishes, and they talked about Christmas.

"If I could have anything," said Rose, "I'd wish for a Christmas tree with more colorful decorations on it than we have ever seen. It would have garland and ornaments and a great big star on top."

"I'd wish for a big plump turkey for the finest Christmas dinner we've ever tasted," Mama said.

Papa chuckled at them. "Looks like Rose isn't the only dreamer in the family," he said. "I can't promise you a turkey, but maybe I can find a nice fat goose for our Christmas dinner."

Papa put on his big coat and his hunting hat. Then he went out the door and headed toward the woods.

In the late afternoon, Papa tramped back into the cabin. He carried a gunnysack over his shoulder. "I didn't see any geese," he said, "but I did bring home a big pheasant."

Papa took the pheasant from the sack and showed it to the family. Then he hung it outside.

"I'll clean it after supper," he said.

But when Rose peeked outside, she saw something much bigger than a pheasant—a bear! "Papa!" she said. "There's a bear eating our Christmas dinner!"

The bear ran off into the woods, and all that was left of the pheasant were a few feathers lying in the grass. Rose sadly wondered what they would do for Christmas dinner.

The next day was Christmas Eve, so Papa didn't waste any time. Again he went hunting. This time he returned with a small quail. He cleaned the quail right away and brought it into the house. He didn't want it to be eaten by any hungry forest creatures.

"It's not very big," said Papa.

"It's exactly big enough," said Mama. "Sarah, you can help me by peeling potatoes and carrots for quail soup. Rose, while I bake a loaf of bread, you can churn some fresh butter. This will be a wonderful meal. Don't worry."

Soon the quail soup simmered in Mama's big kettle on the stove. Rose and her brothers and sisters giggled excitedly. Mama's meals were always delicious.

When dinner was ready, Rose and her family gathered around the table. They bowed their heads to give thanks.

Rose looked up when she heard a *tap-tap-tap.* Someone was knocking on the cabin door.

Papa opened the door, and a stranger stood on the step. "Can you shelter a tired and hungry traveler from the cold?" the stranger asked.

Papa helped the old man inside, and Mama set an extra place at the table for him. When she had ladled out bowls of soup for everyone, the kettle was completely empty.

"We have just enough," Mama said with a smile as she sat down to eat.

After dinner, the stranger pulled a harmonica from his pocket and began to play it. Papa kicked the rug aside, and soon everyone was dancing.

Finally Mama announced that it was time for bed. James and Henry piled lots of blankets on the floor for the stranger. Then everyone went to sleep.

But before Rose closed her eyes, she took another peek out the window. She saw a bright yellow star shooting across the night sky.

"Please let my family have a great Christmas Day," she whispered, wishing on the star.

When Rose awoke the next morning, the stranger was gone. But on the floor where he had slept, there were many presents. The family could not believe it.

Mama unwrapped a beautiful green dress, and Papa opened a shiny, black pipe. James and Henry unwrapped wool coats, and Sarah unwrapped a rocking horse. There was even a crib for Baby Bonnie.

Rose thought the stranger had forgotten her until she glanced outside. There stood a glorious Christmas tree with garland, ornaments, and a big star on top!

"It's a Christmas miracle!" cried Rose. "Merry Christmas!"

A Christmas Carol

Adapted by Guy Davis
Illustrated by Diana Magnuson

Ebenezer Scrooge was in a very bad mood, but then again, Scrooge was always in a very bad mood.

"Bah! Humbug!" Scrooge said.

Ebenezer Scrooge was a greedy, bitter old man who only cared about his money. He happened to be in an especially bad mood because the next day was Christmas. Scrooge hated the idea of giving to others, so it was only natural that he hated anything to do with Christmas.

"Go away!" Scrooge yelled at some Christmas carolers. "Go and sing your foolish songs somewhere else! We're trying to work here!"

Scrooge glared across his desk at his clerk, Bob Cratchit. “I suppose you will want the whole day off tomorrow?” asked Scrooge.

“Thank you, Mr. Scrooge,” replied Cratchit. “That would be wonderful! My family will enjoy the day together, and we’ll give thanks for our many blessings!”

“What do you have to be thankful for?” mumbled Scrooge, as Cratchit hurried home to his family to prepare for Christmas. “You’re as poor as a mouse!”

Still in a very bad mood, Scrooge put on his coat and went home through the snowy night.

Later that night, Scrooge woke up with a fright. There was a ghost in his bedroom! It was Jacob Marley, Scrooge's old business partner.

"Marley, what are you doing here?" asked a scared and confused Scrooge.

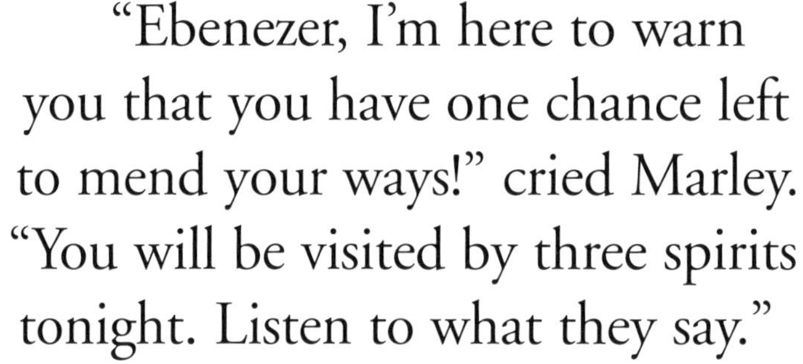

"Ebenezer, I'm here to warn you that you have one chance left to mend your ways!" cried Marley. "You will be visited by three spirits tonight. Listen to what they say."

In a flash, Marley's ghost was gone. But before Scrooge could fall asleep again, he was greeted by another ghost.

"Who are you?" asked an upset Scrooge. "What are you doing in my bed chamber? What is it that you want?"

"I am the Ghost of Christmas Past," said the young-looking spirit. "Come with me, Scrooge."

The ghost took Scrooge to several scenes from Scrooge's past. Each time, Scrooge saw himself as a lonely person who only cared about money. Suddenly, Scrooge found himself in a garden listening to the woman to whom he had once been engaged. The woman was very sad. She said good-bye to Scrooge because she knew he loved his money more than he loved her.

Scrooge sadly watched as the love of his life walked away. The memory was devastating for the old man.

"Haunt me no more, dreadful spirit," said Scrooge. "Take me away from this horrible nightmare!"

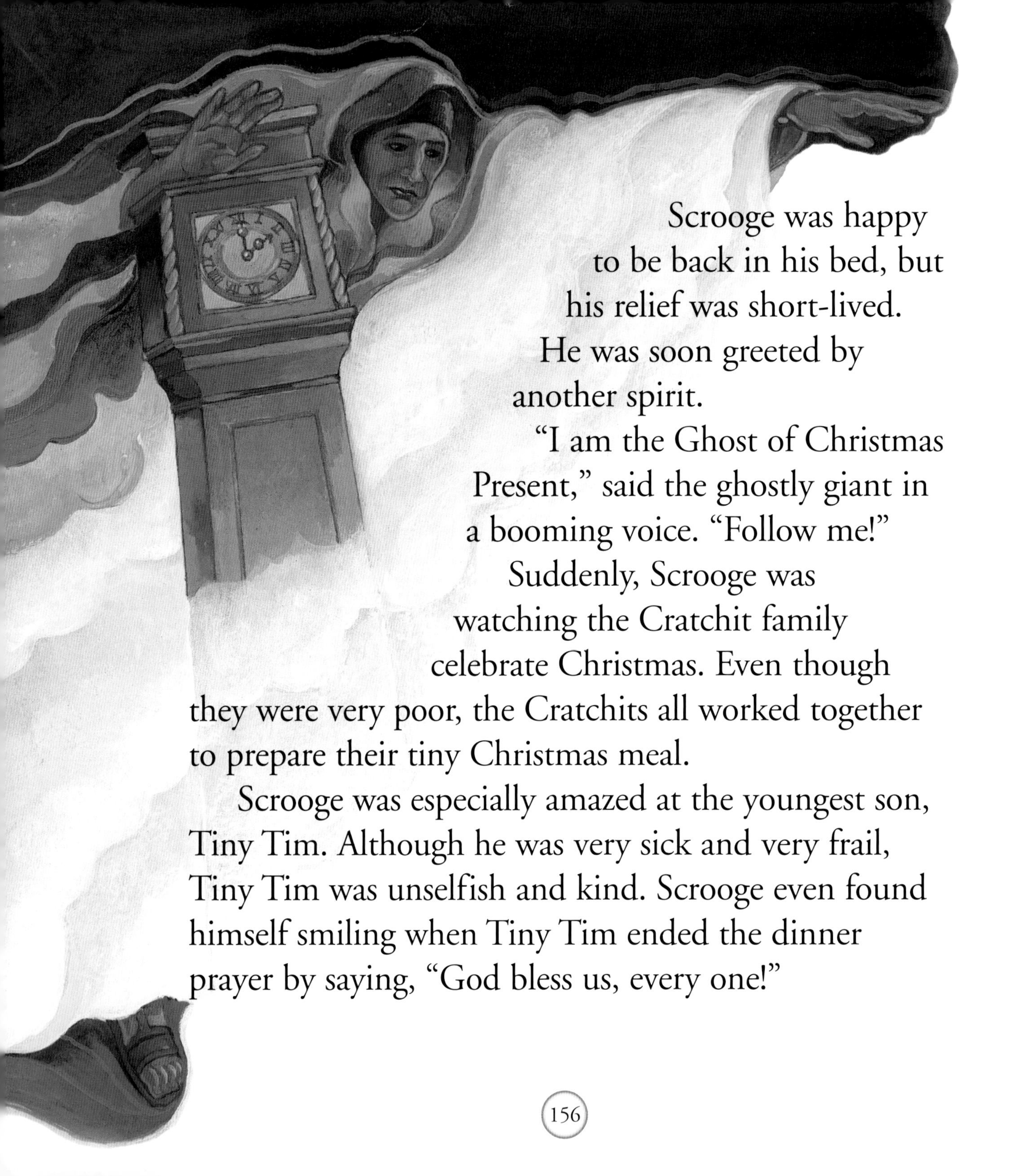

Scrooge was happy to be back in his bed, but his relief was short-lived. He was soon greeted by another spirit.

"I am the Ghost of Christmas Present," said the ghostly giant in a booming voice. "Follow me!"

Suddenly, Scrooge was watching the Cratchit family celebrate Christmas. Even though they were very poor, the Cratchits all worked together to prepare their tiny Christmas meal.

Scrooge was especially amazed at the youngest son, Tiny Tim. Although he was very sick and very frail, Tiny Tim was unselfish and kind. Scrooge even found himself smiling when Tiny Tim ended the dinner prayer by saying, "God bless us, every one!"

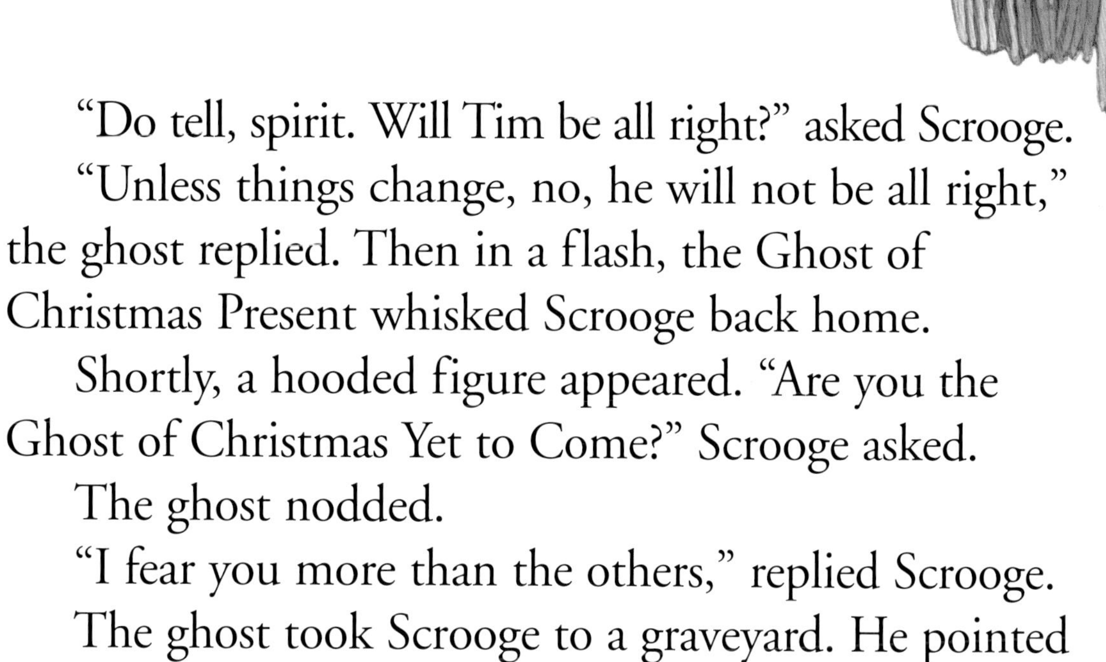

"Do tell, spirit. Will Tim be all right?" asked Scrooge.

"Unless things change, no, he will not be all right," the ghost replied. Then in a flash, the Ghost of Christmas Present whisked Scrooge back home.

Shortly, a hooded figure appeared. "Are you the Ghost of Christmas Yet to Come?" Scrooge asked.

The ghost nodded.

"I fear you more than the others," replied Scrooge.

The ghost took Scrooge to a graveyard. He pointed at a neglected gravestone that was covered with weeds. The name chiseled on the gravestone read "Ebenezer Scrooge."

"What about Tiny Tim?" asked Scrooge fearfully. The ghost took Scrooge to the Cratchit home, where Bob Cratchit was praying at Tiny Tim's bedside.

Scrooge was very upset at the sight. "Tiny Tim is so sick," said Scrooge. "Maybe things would have turned out different if he could have seen a doctor. If only I had paid Cratchit more money, he could have taken better care of Tiny Tim."

"Please don't let this be the future, spirit!" begged Scrooge. "Let me have another chance!"

Suddenly, Scrooge found himself back in his own bed. With great relief, he ran to the window and threw it open. It was morning!

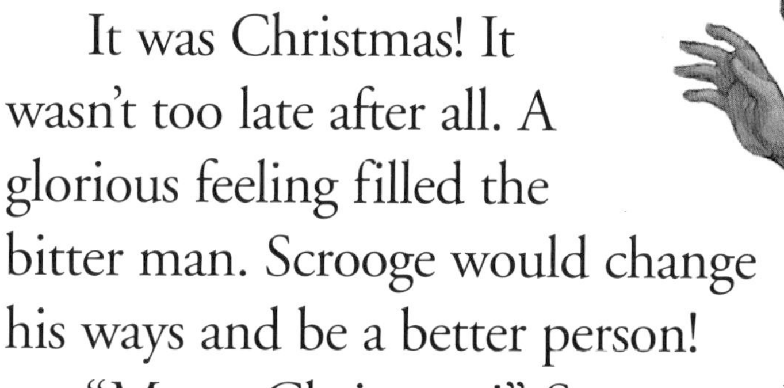

It was Christmas! It wasn't too late after all. A glorious feeling filled the bitter man. Scrooge would change his ways and be a better person!

"Merry Christmas!" Scrooge called from the window to a young boy. Tossing down a bag of coins, Scrooge asked the boy to buy the biggest turkey he could find and take it to the Cratchit family. Scrooge was going to give the Cratchits their best Christmas ever!

Scrooge was grateful to Marley and the three ghosts for helping him make things right. Scrooge knew he would keep Christmas in his heart—not just on Christmas Day but on every day.

"God bless us, every one!" said Scrooge.

Merry Christmas!